What is a hero?

A hero does not wear a cape or mask

Three dog tags his claim to fame

He does not conquer aliens

Defending his country is his aim

Fast cars and lots of money

A true hero rarely has

Instead he is modest, quiet and almost shy

That's a real hero, a man just like my dad

My name is Niamh (but my friends often call me Pud or Nemo), and I am 11 years old. I live in a house with my mummy and three other people. The man that my mummy is a carer for, he is called Tony, his daughter Grace and son Joey.

I also have a big brother called Danny but he does not live with us anymore.

We live in a small village in Cambridgeshire and I go to Brington School. Joey is a little younger than me and is in my class and Grace is two years older. She is bossy and a bully but I guess all big brothers and sisters are.

Even though mummy and Tony are not married they are friends and have decided to live like a family but without the mummy daddy bits.

When I first met Tony I think I was about seven or eight; he was homeless and my mummy worked for a charity that helped people from the Army Navy and Air Force.

He was very poorly; he was really, really thin. He had scars all over his arms; he was very quiet and shaking all the time. Mummy used to take him food and watch him until she was sure that he had eaten it all, and then she would wait with him. They sometimes talked for hours but spent more time just sitting with each other in silence.

At first I did not understand why, but now as I am getting older everything is becoming much clearer.

I did not like this big tall man at first because he scared me. My father was nasty and hurtful so I did not want me or my mummy getting hurt by another person ever again.

If I was asked to do something Tony would always tell me to do it nice or do it twice, and would always tell me that his children were great.

He had spent hours teaching them loads of things and made learning fun. He taught them to count with jelly beans or pennies and explained what he was doing all the time.

My real father never spent any time with me or Danny and would rather go out with his friends.

He never offered to help with our homework or tried to join in with the things that we liked to do. My mum was the person who worked every day and came home to look us all. We went out with mum and on holiday with her, all the sports days at school and special events were with mum.

Tony took his children out every Saturday morning after working as a lorry driver all week. They would go off-roading in their truck or go to the market and buy sweets and have a bacon sandwich.

Grace had won an award at school; Joe was brilliant at maths and science and represented his school in some competition. They were both really good at maths and were ultra clever at English; I wasn't that good at anything and I had never done anything Tony thought was good. I had always found school difficult and got mixed

up with my spellings, words and stuff.

I was quite good at sports though and played rugby, football, basketball, and even cross country running for my school, but this did not seem to matter to Tony.

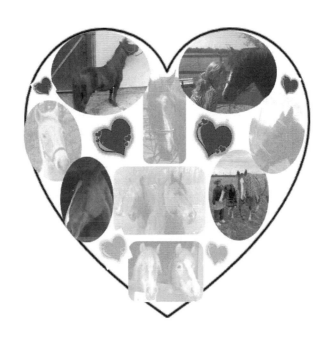

Before mum had met Tony, I qualified for the Horse of the Year Show after three shows and no riding lessons; so there! Mum always says that it was a talented horse, but hey!

Tony had taken his children on loads of holidays and they had done tonnes of things together.

Maybe I was jealous, I don't know, but I was not happy. I did not hate him but I did not want to be friends with this man either.

Mummy would sit with Tony for hours and hours talking and trying to encourage him to do things that he was good at. She would tell him to make garden furniture in his little shed, paint colourful pictures and work around the garden.

He was so, so clever and made all sorts of things out of bits of wood. His pictures were of often places he had been to in France.

Even though he was so clever and could do loads of great things his eyes were always sad and he never ever smiled.

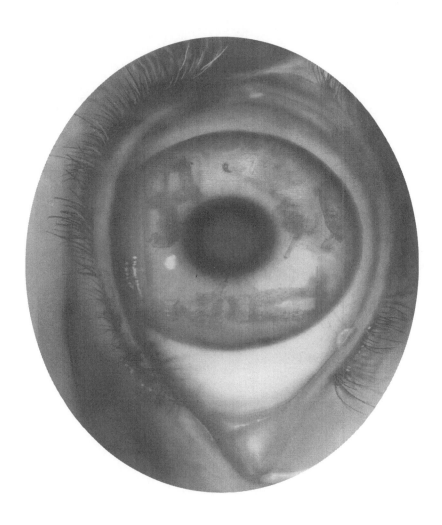

I remember mummy collecting my big brother Danny from school one day; and stopping outside our house. She asked us to get out and said she had to go and see Tony, she did not know why but she knew something was wrong.

We went to stay with our Aunt and Uncle and were told later that he had taken an overdose.

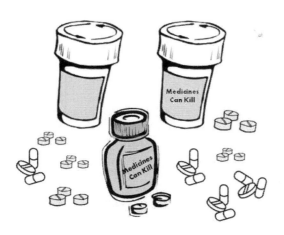

From what mummy told us when she got to his house the doors were locked, all the food had been thrown in the bin, everything was laid out neatly and phones were unplugged. His ex-wife had told him he would never see his kids again.

At the time I did not understand how much a comment like that this meant to Tony as my father had left home the year before and never even phoned.

I was glad because he was a bully. I was happy at the thought of never having to see him again.

When Tony left hospital mummy became his carer and gave up her voluntary work to look after him.

She started to bring him over to see our horses and he fell in love with Honey.

He learnt to ride and I started to like him, he did not shout or scream at me like my Father did and did not hit or threaten me.

He was starting to become ok. He made me some jumps for my horses and would even go out for a hack with me.

Grace and Joe used to come to my house and I helped them to learn about horses, Grace would ride on my pony Polo and I would take Freddie out; Joe would also ride but enjoyed shooting targets in the barns and exploring the fields with his friends more.

They would both cry and get upset when their mum used to come and collect them screaming that they wanted to stay with their Daddy. This really upset Tony and it often made him cry too.

Their mum would shout and say that "No court in the land would let a man have custody of children over a mother, especially not one who is mentally ill". She would scream and shout at all of them and even pushed my Mum out of the way to snatch her daughter. She frightened me and reminded me of my father, a bully.

How could this person say such bad

things   , Tony
was always so kind and gentle,
everything my Father wasn't. Any

child in the land would be lucky to have such a great dad.

Tony would often cry and I did not know why, he did not like to go out and hated being around lots of people.

He became more and more ill and mummy needed to help him more. He would not speak to any of us for days and days or be really grumpy even if we were doing something really nice.

I did not understand why we were always upsetting him, why did he not like us. I thought that he did not like me and Danny because he did not see Joe and Grace much.

Things have changed so much since then, I am eleven now and life is soooo very different.

As I said we all live in a small village in Cambridgeshire and we are a sort of family. Grace and Joe and me would all like Tony and mummy to fall in love and get married, then we could be a proper family. Grace even asked if mum could have a baby or adopt.

Mummy keeps explaining that they are best of friends and that is all so I am not going to be a bridesmaid and neither is Grace and neither of us will be a big sister to a baby.

Joe is a boy and even though he is a pain, cus all boys are, he is really kind and when Grace picks on us we both hide in his room.

He is like a little brother and loves to play with soldiers and action men. I still love my horses.

Grace and Joey call my Mummy, mum and I call Tony Daddy. He is like a daddy to me. He helps me with my homework and listens to me when I get upset.

Tony, daddy, is not like a normal daddy and this is what I want to tell you about. Pssst! I don't think Grace likes me calling her Daddy that but I let her share my mummy so it is only fair.

It is silly but Daddy was in the Army and has done lots of things in lots of countries. Mummy sits up and watches him all night because he screams in his sleep and cries.

He gets up and "patrols" around the house before settling back down to sleep again.

If you touch him when he is asleep he will throw his arms out and try to hit you because he does not know it is us.

When we go out Daddy will look on roofs and totally ignore us, we know that he is looking for something but don't know what it is about. He will check the car before we go anywhere and spots everything unusual.

If a car has been behind us for a long way he will tell us and then let us know the registration number. If an odd car is parked on the road he will keep an eye on it.

In shops he will change and start to panic when he hears foreign voices. He does not say anything, he just wants to leave and starts to look for the way out.

Babies crying or screaming, we have to leave; lots and lots of people; we have to leave. We have to be careful where we go out because loads of places make Daddy upset and ill.

Firework night is horrible. The sound of fireworks can make a big tall man drop to the floor curled up in a small ball crying and shaking.

If there is a loud bang or a car back fires the same thing, a shaking crying man.

People take the mickey out of Joe and me and say that our daddy is a freak because he does not like doing daddy things. He cannot take us to the park, partly because he has a bad back and bad legs but also because he has a poorly head.

People cannot see that he is poorly and think that he is lazy. They do not understand that sounds and smells can upset him. I don't know why but the smell of marzipan or almonds will make him shiver, he hates watching the news and lots of programmes make him panic.

We often have weeks when he does not speak to us; it can be for day and days or for weeks and weeks. Other weeks he will be really snappy and shout at us for silly things. Sometimes he will not want a hug and kiss goodnight.

We all know now that he does not mean to be like this, he is ill, but it is still horrible.

Even special days like Christmas or birthdays don't make him smile, his eyes are always sad even when he says that he is happy.

It really hurts when he and mummy shout at each other, it makes us feel like we have done something wrong or that we are bad children.

It makes us all sad that we cannot just run over and give our Daddy a hug whenever we want, and that our shouting and screaming can upset him. We cannot go to theme parks with him because he cannot cope with crowds and do lots of things that our friends do.

People, even adults cannot understand why my mummy has to look after Daddy in the day and night; because they cannot see anything wrong with him at a glance, they cannot see the battles in his head so they are horrible and tell him he is not ill.

He is frightened to wear his medals because people tell him he is too young to have got so many and make him feel bad.

I am lucky that he has never hit me when he has a nightmare but I know that he grabbed Joey round the throat, not knowing it was his little boy and thinking that he was being attacked. He would never ever hurt any of us, but does not always know where he is or what he is doing.

He goes to a place called Combat Stress and gets help for his poorly head.

The people there are lovely and do not mind us going to visit him.

Some people there have lost their friends and family because they have been poorly and not understood what the matter is.

My daddy is a really special man but

he is ill. I am learning to understand that it is an illness and he cannot help the way he is but I still don't understand why.

If you are lucky you will have "normal parents", maybe step mums and dads and maybe even step brothers and sisters.

Maybe you also have a mum or dad that isn't quite like your friends. You may have someone in your family who has a birth mark, a scar or is perhaps in a wheelchair, that does not make you or them a freak and you should hold your head up high.

You and your family are as perfect

as anyone else.

My Daddy has PTSD and even though I don't understand it, I am

Mood swings
Cold sweats
Anxiety
Depression
Hyper alertness
Night terrors
Panic attacks
Isolation
Loneliness
Nausea
Flashbacks
Withdrawal

Just because you cannot always see mental illness it does not mean that it does not exist. People believe in God, but who has ever seen him/her learning and I know that this is what makes my daddy really special.

I don't mind talking to people about it and if you are like me, Grace and Joe you will learn that it is ok to tell people that members of your family are not "normal" and are ill either in their bodies or their heads, but what is normal.

As a kid there is nothing wrong with asking questions, asking why mum or dad seems sad and asking if you have done something bad.

We have learnt that if we don't ask we don't learn, but there are times when we don't get answers and that is ok too.

No family is perfect and we all have things that we are mega embarrassed about.

I wrote this book to try to let other kids know that it is ok to live in a family that is different to their friends.

Well like all kids I have friends to meet and loads of things to do...

So see you later.

Niamh xx

A thank you to the veteran who gave up his time and prepared the artwork for me.

Bob Langhorn was born in London and grew up in Essex. He joined the Grenadier Guards after leaving school. When his Army career had finished he decided to join the ATC as an Adult Sergeant Instructor and moved to Liverpool.

Bob was diagnosed as having PTSD in 2011 after an incident at work exasperated his symptoms.

I would like to thank Bob for taking time out of his life to work on the illustrations for my books. I am truly flattered that you said you "would be honoured to help as you did not know of many kids who feel so strongly about PTSD"; I am more honoured that any veteran would do such truly fantastic artwork for a kid who wrote down her thoughts.

Can't wait for the rest.

A thank you must also go to Pati Robins. A talented photographer who kindly offered some of her amazing photographs for my books.

Pati is married to a veteran who suffers from PTSD and who was one of my Daddy's troopers.

All of her work is brilliant and well worth a look.

http://probinsphotography.weebly.com

I know that I am only a kid and that my books will never be best sellers; but it is people like my dad who is my inspiration, Bob and Pati that make me feel as though my writing has meaning.

My final word, well for now at least!

I did not write these books to become famous and I am not hoping to make millions of pounds so I am giving all the proceeds to charities that are special to me.

I also started a blog when I realised that kids were reading my books and wanted to get in touch, please feel free to check it out.

http://notesfromniamh.weebly.com

There is also a facebook group that you are welcome to join

http://www.facebook.com/groups/an otefromniamh

I enjoy hearing from other people who have special families.

When I first wrote down my story I thought people would laugh. It is nice to know that I am not alone too